HI, THERE – I'm Patty Mills.

I play basketball in the NBA, and I've represented Australia at the Olympics three times. That's these days. Growing up, I was a sports-loving kid just like you. And that's why I'm excited about my new series of kids' books, Game Day!

Patty, the main character, loves playing every sport he can – especially basketball. He learns many important skills and values through sports, dancing, and of course, at school. He also has a whole lot of fun with his friends, but when it comes to game day, he always makes sure he's ready to perform.

I think you're going to love taking this journey with Patty. Have fun reading the series, don't miss the glossary in the back of every book, and I hope to see you on the basketball court one day!

THE GAME DAY! SERIES

BOOK 1 *Patty Hits the Court*

BOOK 2 *Patty and the Shadows*

BOOK 3 *Patty Takes Charge*

First American Edition 2020
Kane Miller, A Division of EDC Publishing

First published in Australia in 2017 by Allen & Unwin.
Cover design by Ruth Grüner and Nahum Ziersch.
Text design and typesetting by Ruth Grüner.
Cover illustration by Nahum Ziersch.

For information contact:
Kane Miller, A Division of EDC Publishing
PO Box 470663
Tulsa, OK 74147-0663
www.kanemiller.com
www.edcpub.com
www.usbornebooksandmore.com

Library of Congress Control Number: 2019940426

Printed and bound in the United States of America

1 2 3 4 5 6 7 8 9 10

ISBN: 978-1-68464-024-9

BOOK 3

PATTY MILLS

WITH JARED THOMAS

ILLUSTRATIONS BY NAHUM ZIERSCH

I DRIBBLED OUT FROM THE KEY, spun and scored.

"Awesome shot, Patty!" Tyson said.

"Let's shut them down now," Boris said as we ran back to defend.

I looked at the clock. There were only two minutes left in the game against St. Joseph's. Scoring another five points to win was a big ask.

I was guarding their ball carrier, and as he tried to get around me, the ball bounced off my foot and out of court.

"Foot violation," the referee called.

I was so frustrated. But Tyson slapped me on the back. "Don't worry about it, Patty," he said. "You were trying your best."

St. Joseph's pulled further ahead of us with a transition jump shot from their point guard. I scored once more, but in the end we couldn't catch them.

Although we lost, there were high fives all around between Tyson, Manu, Boris, Ben, Tiago and me. My best mate, Josie, was missing, and I had no idea where she was.

As everyone headed for their drink bottles,

Coach Clarke said, "Patty, Tyson and Manu, can I have a word with you?"

Oh man, I thought. I was worried that Coach Clarke might start telling Tyson and me how pleased he was we were getting on and mess things up. Tyson had been my rival since I could remember. Apart from footy, he had beaten me at almost everything, until the beginning of the year when I grew a couple of inches and got a lot faster and stronger. But we'd been teammates for a while now, and we were finally starting to support each other.

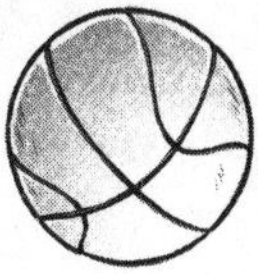

"What's up, Coach?" I asked.

"I've got good news," he said, tucking the basketball beneath his arm. "The three of you have been selected to represent Canberra in the

East Coast under-twelves basketball tournament."

"Awesome!" Tyson said, a huge grin on his face.

"Really? Wow!" Manu said, putting his hand to his head as if something had just hit him.

"You've been selected as the best players in your age group. You should be very proud of yourselves," Coach Clarke told us.

I was over the moon. Basketball had become so important to me, and for the first time I thought I might really have a future in it. But I had one question. “Will I still be able to play with the Shadows?”

“Yes, of course,” Coach Clarke said. “The tournament is being played during the holidays at Sydney Olympic Park Stadium. You'll love it.”

Tyson was bouncing around, full of excitement and energy as we headed back to the school bus. “I knew you'd make the team, Manu,” he said. “But I can't believe both of us did too, Patty. I thought it'd come down to just one of us.”

“It's unreal,” I told him.

"HEY, JOSIE!" I called out. I saw her shooting hoops in the park as I walked home from school.

I threw my backpack down next to the court and jumped in front of her to catch the rebound.

"Where were you today?" I asked.

"I had to go to the doctor."

"Is everything all right?"

"I thought I was dying. But the doctor said

it was only growing pains. Who won the game?"

I told her all about our match with St. Joseph's. "But I have some good news too," I said. "Coach Clarke told me I've made the under-twelves team to represent Canberra in some tournament during the holidays."

Josie's eyes opened wide. "It's not just some tournament, Patty. It's the East Coast under-twelves basketball tournament!"

"Yeah, I know," I answered, a smile spreading across my face.

"That's awesome! But what about the trip to the Torres Strait for your Athe's birthday?"

Athe is what we call our granddads in the central and western islands of the Torres Strait. I felt guilty and confused because I'd forgotten all about my Athe's fiftieth birthday celebrations. All our family and friends, including Josie's family, would be there.

I sat down on the basketball and said, "All I think about is basketball and being with my family in the Torres Strait, and I don't know which I love more."

Josie sat down in front of me and said, "Patty, I know you love the Torres Strait—"

My mind went straight to the islands, where the weather is warm, everyone is nice, and the food is delicious. Not to mention how much I love being surrounded by my family.

"But like I said," Josie went on, "it's always going to be there. And maybe there's some way you can play in the tournament *and* go to the Torres Strait for your Athe's party."

I thought about what Josie said, but I knew that the only way I could play in the tournament was to miss out on some time in the Torres Strait.

"Let's play one-on-one," I said, jumping up from the court.

I WAS PUSHING A CART around the supermarket with Mum and Dad, thinking about what it would be like to play in a tournament with Tyson. Would he start to annoy me again?

As we walked down the treats aisle, I didn't even hear Dad when he asked, "What type of chocolate should we get, Patty?"

"Whatever, I don't mind," I said, beginning

to think about how my cousins would react if I missed a week with them in the Torres Strait because I was playing basketball in Sydney.

"Are you okay?" Dad asked, giving me a strange look.

"Yes, I'm fine," I said absently.

After we went through the checkout I started walking to the parking lot, but Mum said, "Patty, we're going this way."

"Where?" I asked.

"The travel agent. We have to book our tickets."

Usually, going to the travel agent with Dad and Mum was the best thing in the world. I loved booking our tickets, making sure that I got a window seat. I'd count down the days until I could feel the warm sun on my back, see my grandparents and all my cousins, go swimming on the reefs with the fish and turtles and head to Uncle Frankie's Café for the best banana milkshake. But all I could think about now was how I was going to tell Coach Clarke that I wouldn't be able to join the team.

The travel agent asked what she could help us with.

"We'd like to fly to the Torres Strait on the twenty-third of September," Dad said. That was just before the tournament. "And return on the eighth of October." That was a week after the tournament.

"Let's see what we can find," the travel agent said, typing away on her keyboard.

I didn't know where to start. I had to tell Mum and Dad about the tournament. I didn't want to miss it *or* going to the Torres Strait.

"Dad," I said, tapping him on the shoulder.

"Yes."

"I've been selected to play basketball for the Canberra representative team."

"That's great, Patty," Dad said, turning his attention back to the travel agent.

"There are flights available, and I've even got a window seat for Patty," the travel agent said.

"Dad and Mum," I said, raising my voice. "The tournament is being played in the first week of the holidays."

Both my parents turned to look at me. The

travel agent smiled at us. “How about you take a bit of time to talk,” she said. “We’re open late tonight, and on the weekend too. Just come back when you’re ready.”

“Thank you,” Mum said. “Yes, I think we need some time to talk.”

DAD AND MUM took me to a café nearby.

“I only found out about it today,” I told them.

“It’s really great,” Mum said. “You should be very proud of yourself.”

“You think so?” I asked, surprised.

“It’s great that you’re making so much progress with your basketball,” Dad said. “All your hard work is paying off."

"But to play in the tournament I'd have to miss out on our holiday and Athe's birthday party."

"Maybe you could join us after the tournament?" Dad said.

"Have Patty catch a plane to the Torres Strait by himself?" Mum asked.

"He's big enough. And we'll all be waiting for him when he arrives. Do you know your Uncle Sam was the first person to leave the Torres Strait to train for basketball at the Australian Institute of Sport?"

I shook my head.

"He was older than you, of course," Dad continued. "But the thing is, sometimes when you want to reach your potential, you need to make sacrifices. Do you want to play in the tournament?"

I was so confused. "I do. But I don't want to miss out on time in the Torres Strait or disappoint Athe," I sighed.

"How about we talk to Coach Clarke and take a day or two to think about it? There'll still be flights available," Mum said.

AT LUNCHTIME, Ms. Kelly walked to the edge of the court and called to Josie. I watched Josie follow her to the staff room. "I'll be back," she said.

It was a tough few minutes for Tyson and me, trying to keep up with Tiago, Boris and Manu without Josie to help us.

She reappeared as we were walking back

to class. “What was that about? Why are you looking so happy?” I asked.

“I’ve been selected to play on the girls’ tournament team.”

“That’s awesome!” I said, giving Josie a high five. “So are you going to play instead of going to the Torres Strait?”

"The solution you and your parents were talking about sounds great to me. A week playing in a basketball tournament and a week in the Torres Strait would be the perfect holiday! As long as my parents agree," Josie said.

"Do you want me to be there when you talk to them?"

"Yeah, thanks, that might help."

JOSIE AND I SAT AROUND our kitchen table as our parents had a cup of tea and talked about the tournament.

It turned out that Athe's birthday was during the first week of the holidays,

when the tournament was being played, and his birthday party was happening the day after the tournament finished.

"Mum and I would love to be there in Sydney to watch you, but we've had a family dinner planned on the day of Athe's actual birthday for a long time," Dad said. "But we think you and Josie could fly up from Sydney together. How does everybody feel about that?"

I looked at Josie's parents, who nodded in agreement. Then I looked to Josie. I could see the relief wash over her face.

"Do you think Athe will be okay with me not being there on his actual birthday?" I said.

Josie's dad laughed and said, "I bet your Athe

wishes he were playing in the tournament with you, Patty."

Dad ruffled my hair and said, "That's right. And you'll still get to celebrate with him. But Mum and I have to be there with Athe on the day of his actual birthday."

"Maybe you can call Athe from Sydney? We need to ask Coach Clarke if he's prepared to take you and Josie to the airport too," Mum said.

AFTER SCHOOL THE NEXT DAY Tyson and I rode to our first representative team training session. We'd never ridden anywhere together before.

I changed up a gear, coasting along on my mountain bike next to Tyson's BMX.

When we walked into the stadium, Matthew, one of Tyson's club basketball teammates from the Titans, was at the far end of the court shooting hoops.

It felt weird walking up to him, knowing that we were going to be playing on the same team. Usually I was sizing his team up from the other end of the court. Matthew was one of the toughest competitors I'd ever been up against. In my first season of school basketball Matthew had demolished us in the semifinal.

As I walked toward Matthew I started to wonder who else might be on our team. I'd been so caught up thinking about whether I'd get to the Torres Strait for the holidays that I hadn't even asked Coach Clarke who else had been selected.

Tyson and I joined Matthew and started shooting hoops. As I was lining up for a

three-pointer, someone slapped me on the back. I turned around to see Luke, my teammate from the Shadows.

"Good to see you, *bala*," Luke said as he shook my hand.

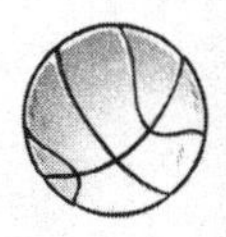

"Good to see you too, *bala*," I said. *Bala* means brother in Torres Strait language.

A few more players from other clubs walked into the stadium with their parents, and a minute later Manu walked in with Coach Clarke.

"Congratulations on being selected to represent Canberra in the East Coast under-twelves basketball tournament," Coach Clarke said. Tyson shot me a smile. "Let's all get to know each other a bit better by sharing how long you've been playing basketball, what you think your strength is, and something you'd like to improve."

"I don't want to give my secrets away," Luke said. "We start playing against these fellas in the club season soon."

"We're on the same team now – no secrets.

And Luke, I already know you need to learn to dribble on your left hand," Coach Clarke said.

Luke laughed and said, "Yeah, but I always get the rebounds."

IT WAS NO WONDER Tyson and Matthew were so good at basketball; they'd been playing since they were seven years old. I'd seen the little kids playing with the hoop lowered before our club games.

"I want you to know that you are all brilliant," Coach Clarke said. "You're the best basketballers for your age in Canberra. But the East Coast tournament is going to test you like you've never been tested before."

My new teammates and I were all concentrating really hard on what Coach Clarke was saying.

"We only have four training sessions together before the tournament," he continued. "Rather than teaching you new drills, I've set you all some to practice in your own time. During our sessions, I want you to focus on the basics."

"I guess you want me to tie my right hand behind my back or something?" Luke asked.

"You've got it," Coach Clarke answered. "I don't want to see you use your right hand during training unless it's absolutely necessary. Tyson, we need to get some pressure around you. Patty and the Shadows forced too many errors from you last season. And Patty, have you been practicing your transition jump shot?"

I hadn't been developing it as much as I knew I should have. So when Coach Clarke let us work on our own areas for improvement at the end of the session, I was determined to work harder than ever.

I was deep in concentration when I leapt into the air. But in the next instant, I felt myself tip off balance. I came down hard on my right ankle.

"Ahhhhh," I screamed.

COACH CLARKE raced over as I held my ankle.

"Are you okay, Patty?"

"I think it's broken."

"Let's have a look."

"Ouch!!" I yelled as Coach Clarke started to untie the laces on my shoe.

Coach finally removed my sock, and I looked down to see my bruised and puffy ankle. I felt like throwing up, it hurt so much.

"Don't move, and I'll get some ice and call your dad," Coach said. My teammates huddled around me.

"Whoa, Patty, that looks really bad," Manu said. His eyes said much more. There was no way I'd be playing in the tournament with a broken ankle.

"WHAT HAVE YOU done to yourself, Patty?" Dr. Sophie asked as she helped me into her office.

"I think I've broken my ankle."

"Let's get you straight up onto the exam table."

I explained to the doctor what had happened and how it felt. Then she gently felt my ankle and rolled my foot around to see what movement it had. "Ouch, ouch, ouch!" I said.

Dr. Sophie released my foot and said, "The good news is, your ankle isn't broken, Patty. It is very badly sprained, however. You'll need lots of rest and to keep icing it."

"So I don't have to wear a cast?"

Dad laughed, and Dr. Sophie said, "No. But I'll give you some crutches to help you get around without putting your weight on it."

I felt relieved, but I was still scared to ask my next question. "Will I be able to play in the basketball tournament next month?"

"It's really hard to say, Patty," Dr. Sophie said. "But the more you rest it and ice it, the greater your chances."

DAD AND MUM SPOILED ME when I got home. They let me lie on the couch and watch television while I ate dinner, and said I could take time off school until I could move around again.

Josie came to visit me the next day. We sat on the couch watching basketball and drinking the banana milkshakes that Mum had made us.

"Man, you're lucky, Patty," Josie said.

"Lucky, with a sprained ankle?" I asked.

"Yeah, you get to do all of the things that I wish I was doing while I'm at school."

"No way. I can't do anything. Even using the crutches to get to my room hurts. It's driving me crazy not being able to run or practice."

"But you can watch all the basketball you want," Josie said, turning her attention back to the television screen.

"Yeah, but it's not the same as playing," I told her.

THE NEXT DAY when Dad and Mum went to work I lay on the couch and watched some more basketball. The only problem was that it made me so desperate to play.

I hobbled to my room to get my ball and then out to the driveway. I stood in front of my basketball hoop, lay my crutches against the wall and stood on one foot to try a three-pointer.

I pushed the ball into the air, forcing it from my shoulder because I couldn't push up through my legs. The ball

went through the hoop, and I hopped over to get it.

I must have taken about five shots before my ankle started throbbing. I went back inside to ice it, worried that I'd hurt it even more.

AFTER A COUPLE of days at home my ankle felt good enough for me to go back to school.

When Tyson first saw me limping to class on my crutches he asked, "Let us have a try, Patty."

I handed my crutches to Tyson.

"They're not easy to get around on, are they?" Tyson said.

I shrugged my shoulders, knowing exactly how hard it was to move around on crutches.

"When will your ankle be better, Patty?" Manu asked.

"I don't know. Dr. Sophie said the more I rest it, the quicker it will heal."

"Well, you better rest," Manu said. "We need you ready for the tournament."

THAT LUNCHTIME, Manu, Boris, Tiago and Josie followed me into the library. "We'll have a board game tournament," Tiago declared.

We played a couple of rounds of Connect Four, but it was hard to concentrate. It was sunny outside, and I could hear everyone playing in the quadrangle, on the oval, and in the playground.

I was grateful that my friends were trying to help entertain me, but I knew they really wanted to get outside and play basketball. I couldn't blame them.

"Go and play for the rest of the break," I told them.

"Are you sure?" Josie asked.

"It's what I'd be doing if I could walk."

"What are you going to do?" Boris asked.

"Read or do homework," I told them.

And that's exactly what I did. I actually enjoyed reading during recess and lunch and was even ahead on my homework.

ONE MORNING I TRIED to stand on my right foot and although it still hurt a little bit, it felt much better. "I'll pick you up after school, and we'll go to see Dr. Sophie," Mum said.

I was glad to see Dr. Sophie. "How's your ankle feeling, Patty?" she asked.

"The bruising has almost disappeared, and it feels heaps stronger."

"That's great," she said. She patted the exam table for me to sit up on it.

I took off my sock and Dr. Sophie started to gently move my foot.

"How does that feel?" she asked.

There was still a little bit of pain, but I told her, “It doesn’t feel too bad.”

“There seems to be a good range of movement. You can start walking on it.”

Mum smiled at me. “Really?” I said.

“But no running!” Dr. Sophie said, waving her finger. “You still have to take it easy. I want you to come back next week, and I’ll check the recovery you’ve made.”

“When can I start training and playing again?” I asked, hopeful that it wouldn’t be long.

“It could be at least two weeks, maybe less – depending on how much you rest.”

It was such a relief to walk out of Dr. Sophie’s office without the crutches.

CHAPTER 8

I TOLD COACH CLARKE that I'd only have to sit out for one training session. I was scared of losing my spot on the team. There were other kids desperate to play in the tournament.

I went along to the next session to watch, and already my ankle was starting to feel like I hadn't sprained it at all. The bruising had almost disappeared, and I was walking fine.

When training finished and Coach Clarke walked over to talk to one of the parents, Manu ran up to me. "Just come and shoot some hoops with us," he said. "You don't have to move around."

I was so sick of watching from the sideline that I couldn't resist. At first I just stood beneath the basket, passing the rebounds back to my team and taking the odd shot. Then, as Tyson approached the basket, without thinking I started to guard, shuffling across to block his path. When he dodged, I followed. And then I felt another sharp pain in my ankle.

The pain took my breath away. I tried to make my way back to the bench without anyone noticing, especially Coach

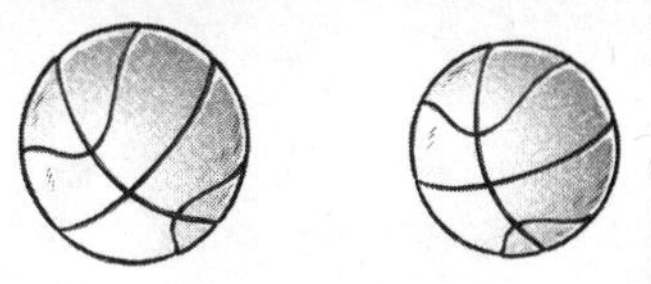

Clarke. I was scared that my chances of playing in the tournament were really ruined this time.

AFTER THAT, I iced and rested my ankle more than ever, and it improved quickly. Dr. Sophie told me to sit out one more training session, and after that I could go back to all my normal activities. I was so relieved.

Mum and Dad and all my teammates' parents were at the last training session. Coach Clarke had organized a barbecue afterward.

Before we hit the court, Coach told me to take it easy, but Dad had strapped my ankle, and it felt fine for the whole session.

When we gathered for dinner afterward, Coach Clarke stood up. "It's time to present you all with your jerseys," he said. He held up a jersey that was white, yellow and blue. It had the number one on it.

"This jersey is for Patty," Coach Clarke said. "Patty has only been playing basketball for a couple of seasons, but he's become one of the fiercest competitors and point guards in the league. He'll be playing point guard in the tournament."

Everyone clapped as I collected my jersey, but I could tell Tyson was disappointed. I guessed that he wanted to wear the number one jersey or be point guard, like he was in the Titans.

But Coach Clarke went on. "And joining Patty as point guard is Tyson." Tyson grinned and tapped my fist as he walked up to collect his jersey. Then it was my turn to be envious because his was the number eight – my favorite number, and the one I wore for the Shadows.

After dinner our team raced back onto the court to play four on four.

As we played, I paid attention to all my teammates' strengths, noticing how much Luke had improved now that he was using his left hand. Being the point guard meant that I was the coach on the court. I needed to be able to make sure that the plays Coach Clarke called happened, and to instruct my team to make plays when needed.

It felt like a big responsibility. But it was awesome knowing that I was going to Sydney to play in my first tournament.

ON SUNDAY MORNING I CHECKED that I'd packed everything I needed. I was getting nervous about traveling to Sydney, and worrying that I would miss Mum and Dad too much. As I zipped up my bag, I looked up at my poster of Cathy Freeman, the Aboriginal runner who won an Olympic gold medal in the four hundred meters in 2000. I thought about all the times she would have had to travel to race meets by herself, and imagined her packing her bags when she was my age. I knew she would have been brave.

Dad and Mum helped double-check that I'd packed everything, then drove me to the stadium, where Coach Clarke was waiting with the bus.

The girls' team was traveling with us, and Josie and some of my teammates were already there.

"You all ready, *bala*?" Luke asked me.

"Yeah, I'm ready," I said, but I still had butterflies in my belly thinking about how my parents were about to fly to the Torres Strait without me.

A man shook Dad's hand and then mine. "I'm Mr. Jones, Matthew's dad," he said, before

storing my bag beneath the bus. "I'll be helping to make sure you kids don't turn Sydney upside down."

When Coach Clarke told us all to board the bus, Dad hugged me. "Good luck, Patty," he said. "Do your best, and have a great time."

Then Mum gave me a kiss and a hug and said, "Don't worry about us. We'll all be waiting for you."

AS SOON AS WE left the suburbs of Canberra I started to forget about Mum and Dad and the Torres Strait.

Luke, Tyson and I sat in the very back seat,

and Josie and our Shadows teammate Riley sat in front of us.

"Hey, check out the kangaroos," Tyson said, pointing out the window. There were two huge boomers bouncing through the bush. "Did I tell you I get Dad to cook me roo now, Patty?" Tyson said.

"Really?" I asked, remembering how Tyson once told me he'd never eat bush tucker.

"Yeah, I love it."

We had a good time on the bus, talking, joking around and checking out the towns we passed through on the trip.

AFTER LUNCH and a break in a park, Coach Clarke told us that Sydney was less than an hour away, and to save some energy. Our first game of the tournament was that afternoon. I didn't know if it was Coach Clarke giving us an order or the excitement of approaching the city, but we all stared out the bus window in silence.

The traffic that built up as we drove into the city made me nervous. There were so many people everywhere. "Check that out," Luke said as we started traveling across the Sydney Harbour Bridge.

"Oh man," I said, feeling a smile spread across my face. It was amazing being up so high and looking over the harbor to the Opera House.

"How cool is that?" I asked Josie.

"That is way cool," Josie replied.

We all jumped off the bus with our backpacks to get changed into our uniforms. The girls were playing at the same time as us, which meant I wouldn't get to see Josie play.

"Let's try to meet up straight after our games," she said.

Our jaws dropped when we walked into the stadium. It was huge, and there were teams playing on at least seven courts.

"Whoa, this is awesome," Matthew said.

Coach Clarke laughed and said, "Come on, let's get ready, our game is in just under forty minutes."

IT FELT AWESOME walking onto the court with my team in the Canberra uniform.

Coach Clarke led us out to start our warm-up. As I made my first layup I felt a twinge in my ankle, but I was sure I was going to be okay.

I checked out our opposition, Northern Beaches, and tried to work out which one of them might be their point guard.

The Northern Beaches players didn't look taller or stronger than us, and I felt confident. I couldn't wait to see how our representative team performed.

Coach Clarke called us together in a huddle. "When you hit the court," he said, "I just want you all to concentrate on clean ball movement, okay? When you start to find each other with ease, then step it up. Our starting lineup is Patty, Luke, Manu, Jamie and Josh."

"Go, Canberra!" Tyson called as we walked out.

At the tip-off, the Northern Beaches player jumped way higher than Manu. Josh and I immediately raced back to defend, but Northern Beaches were super quick. Two of their players shot around us and scored.

"Come on, Canberra!" Bruce called out, standing up from the bench and clapping his hands.

Jamie passed the ball to me, and all I could think about was passing it on to Manu and Luke, but two of the Northern Beaches players pressured me hard. I got a pass off to Luke, and he dribbled the ball down to our key, but when Josh shot, their center jumped and slapped the ball to one of his teammates. The Northern Beaches players raced down to score another easy basket.

I realized that I was playing against the strongest competition I'd ever faced.

Coach Clarke called time-out. Northern Beaches were on twelve points, and we hadn't even scored.

Coach Clarke subbed off Jamie and Josh for the tall and solid Bruce, and Tyson.

I was glad to have Tyson on the court for his pace and skill. We started scoring, but Northern Beaches were annihilating us.

When the final buzzer went, I looked up at the scoreboard. We'd been beaten by twenty points.

And the worst thing was that I had no idea if the other teams we'd come up against would be just as strong, or even stronger than Northern Beaches.

The only positive I could think of was that I didn't feel my injury the whole way through the game. I thought maybe it was going to be fine.

WE ALL WENT OUT for pizza before heading back to our accommodation. We were staying at a Catholic boarding school across the harbor from the stadium.

"Patty, this place looks haunted," Luke said, the color rushing out of his face as Matthew's dad drove us into the school grounds. The main building

looked like an ancient castle towering before us.

Once we'd unpacked, got into our pajamas and jumped into our bunk beds, Coach Clarke and Mr. Jones came to our door and said, "Lights-out, fellas. We've got a free day tomorrow and there's a lot to fit in."

"Where are we going?" Luke asked.

"If we tell you that it won't be a surprise," Matthew's dad said.

"Night, fellas, and no chatting," Coach Clarke said. He switched off the light.

I tried to get comfortable in the unfamiliar bed, wanting to get some sleep, but also thinking about our defeat in the first game. Then my mind went to Mum and Dad. I knew they would have been feasting with my family on Athe's fish and special vegetables and banana cooked in coconut milk, that we call *sube sube* banana.

My eyelids were finally growing heavy when I noticed a light glowing. I peered over to the bottom bunk. Below me, Tyson had a flashlight held under his chin.

"Cut it out, Tyson," I said.

"But I just remembered, this is the school that had the meanest principal in history."

"What?" Luke asked from the dark on the other side of the room.

"It was a long time ago. But they say the ghosts of the students he terrorized still haunt the corridors."

"Tyson, cut it out," I told him again. I just wanted to get to sleep.

"You're just worried you'll start crying, Patty," Tyson teased, making Bruce giggle.

"I'm tired," I sighed.

"I bet you don't even know any scary stories," Tyson said.

"I don't need to make them up like you do," I answered. This was a mistake. Tyson shone his flashlight at me and asked, "What's the scariest thing you've seen then, Patty?"

I propped myself up on my elbow. Some of the others had turned on their flashlights and I could tell they were all listening.

"It was when I was fishing with my uncle and my big cousin."

"Where?" Bruce asked.

"The Torres Strait."

"Where's that?" Josh asked.

"Off the coast of Queensland, not far from Papua New Guinea," Luke replied.

"We were in my uncle's dinghy, drifting over the reef," I continued. "I had a line in the water, fishing for snapper. My cousin was diving, looking for crayfish."

"To eat?" Jamie asked.

"Yep," I said.

"I bet they're tasty too," Tyson said. "But this story isn't really that scary, Patty."

"It was when two sharks started circling my cousin."

"How big were they?" Tyson asked.

"Much bigger than my cousin," I told him.

"That's crazy," Luke said. "Those reef sharks are fierce."

"Uncle stood up in the dinghy to get a better look. But he didn't call out. My cousin was still diving, with no idea what was going on – I guess my uncle didn't want him to panic. Instead, my uncle sat back down and ripped off his shirt. He said, 'Patty, I'm going in.'

"I looked at the outboard motor nervously, not knowing if I could start it myself if I needed to get help. 'But what if the sharks get you both?' I asked.

"My Uncle looked at me and nodded. 'You'll know what to do. It'll be all right,' he said with a firm voice."

"Oh man, and what did the sharks do when your uncle jumped in?" Jamie asked.

"The sharks kept circling my cousin, but when my uncle got close they backed off a little bit. He must have distracted or confused them. And then my uncle grabbed my cousin by the arm, and my cousin finally realized what was happening. I called out, 'Swim!' But as my uncle and cousin started swimming back toward the boat, calmly at first, the sharks turned on them again."

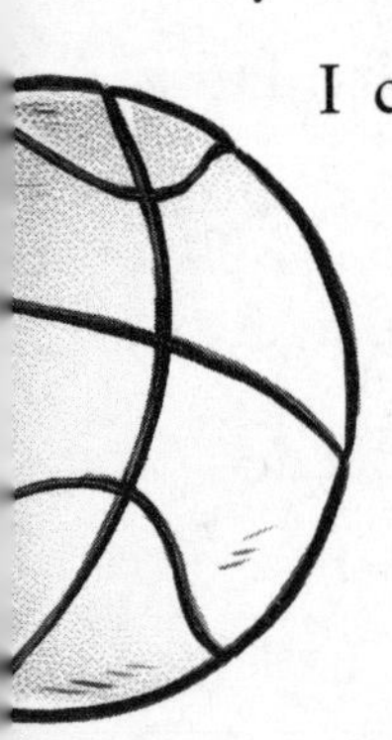

"And did anyone get eaten?" Tyson asked.

"The sharks started moving faster, and I thought my uncle and cousin were goners for sure. But they made it to the boat just in time. One of the sharks took a bite out of my cousin's flipper. Missed his toes by less than two centimeters."

"That is crazy!" Bruce yelled. A moment later, we all shut up when we heard someone walking toward our room.

"No chatting," Coach Clarke said. "You need to rest up if you want to do better in our next game!"

Everyone was silent after that, and I could finally get some sleep.

THE DINING HALL of the boarding school felt huge and empty, even with the entire Canberra team eating breakfast in it. Everyone was quiet as we ate our cereal and toast. I thought about how noisy it must get when the school's boarders shuffled into the hall for their breakfast.

We were all excited piling onto the bus. We headed back toward the city, the driver taking us across the Sydney Harbour Bridge so that we could take in the view across to the Opera House, the ferries, and Luna Park.

Finally, the bus parked near a wharf. "I know this place," Riley said.

"What is it?" I asked.

"It's the Sydney Aquarium," she answered, her eyes bright with excitement.

I felt at home as soon as I spotted the huge floor-to-ceiling tank full of tropical fish.

Tyson grabbed me by the arm. "Come and check this out, Patty."

He led me into a huge tube with water all around it that made me feel like I was on the bottom of the ocean.

"Check them out," Tyson said, but there was

no way that I could miss the massive reef sharks gliding toward us.

"Man, your uncle and cousin were lucky to get away that day," Tyson said.

The whole team stood watching the sharks, stingrays, turtles and giant fish for ages. It was a smaller tank that fascinated me most though.

I sat in front of it, mesmerized by the octopuses unfurling their tentacles and changing color, camouflaging themselves as they moved between rock, reef and plants in their tank.

"Come on, Patty," Coach Clarke said. "It's time for lunch."

In the afternoon we went swimming in the surf at Bondi Beach. And as I drifted off to sleep that night, without Tyson trying to scare us with spooky stories, I thought about the reef sharks and the octopuses.

I remembered Dad telling me that Uncle Sam wore the number eight on his jersey because an octopus has eight arms, and Uncle Sam wished he had eight arms when he was playing basketball. I knew exactly how he felt.

I slept well that night, which was lucky

because we were playing two games the next day. I made sure to strap my ankle.

When we were traveling to the stadium, Luke asked, "How are we going to play better than our last game?"

"Yeah, I don't want to get thrashed again," Tyson said.

"We can play better than we did against Northern Beaches, for starters."

"Obviously," Tyson said, rolling his eyes.

"What I mean is that we had a bad game. We're better than that."

"But what if we're five minutes into the game and getting thrashed again?" Tyson asked. I noticed that Matthew, Bruce, Josh and Jamie were all listening. I thought about what Coach

Clarke would say. "We don't let it rattle us. Stay confident, and focus on good communication and timing."

I might have told my teammates to be confident, but when I entered the stadium and saw the other teams, I wondered if there were any among them that we might be able to beat.

AS WE WERE warming up, Coach Clarke called me aside. "How's your ankle feeling, Patty?"

"It's fine," I told him, "but I'm nervous. We're all worried about getting thrashed again."

Coach Clarke looked around and said, "All

these teams look strong – but they don't know what we're capable of."

"And we don't know what they're capable of," I answered.

"That's where self-belief is most important. You guys know what you can do, you just need to make it happen on the court. Even when you're down, you need to believe that you can turn the game around." I nodded. "Patty, I want you to set the example for your teammates."

THE WESTERN SYDNEY WARRIORS were tall and solid, even towering over Matthew. They were our age, but they looked like full-grown men. Their point guard was the only player on the team that was about my size.

Their center won the tip-off, and before we knew it they were eight points ahead. It felt like our first game of the tournament all over again.

But when I looked over to Coach Clarke, he looked relaxed. He just nodded, reminding me of what I had to do.

When I made the first shot I heard Coach Clarke yell from the bench, “Yes, Patty!”

Luke patted me on the back and said, “Nice one, *bala*.”

“Let’s be strong in defense now, Canberra,” I told my teammates. But within minutes, Western Sydney had scored again.

Coach Clarke called a time-out. Before the coach could speak, Matthew said, “They’re like sharks!”

“So, we need to distract them, don’t we?” Tyson replied. “Like Patty’s uncle when the sharks were after his cousin.”

Coach Clarke looked confused, but glad that our spirits were up. He quickly instructed us. "You need to create space to receive passes and make clear shots, and apply as much pressure as possible in defense."

We started scoring, but the Western Sydney Warriors still beat us by ten points.

After Coach Clarke had talked with us about our game, we ate lunch in the cafeteria. Josie reported that her team had won easily. She'd scored sixteen points. I felt like my team was letting Canberra down.

I turned to Coach Clarke and asked, "Can we work on a few things before our next game?"

"What things?" he asked.

I'd been thinking about the difference

between the Shadows and our Canberra team. Sure, we ran fast breaks when there was opportunity, but we weren't running set plays. I knew that I had to talk with my team about strategy – but that meant giving away secrets about the set plays I ran with the Shadows. I'd have to work on all new set plays when I played against my Canberra teammates during the club season!

I decided that I'd speak to Luke, Josie and Riley to see what they thought. If they were happy for me to share the set plays, I'd get everyone practicing them back at the boarding school.

AS MUCH AS I WANTED to get started teaching my teammates the set plays, we still had one more game that day, and not much time before it started. I decided to put a bit more effort into encouraging my teammates by speaking to them all individually.

"Forget about our last two games," I told Manu and Matthew.

"All that matters is how we play this game."

"We both need to run as hard as we can," I told Tyson.

"We've got this one, *bala*," I said with confidence to Luke as he took a moment to size up the Sydney players.

Luke scratched his head. "They look like men."

"Can you beat your dad at one-on-one?" I asked him.

"Yeah," he said with a nod and a smile.

"Well, let's go." We tapped fists.

COACH CLARKE WALKED WITH US under the basket and said, "If we can win this one, we still stand a chance of making the finals. If we lose, tomorrow is going to be a very tough day. Patty, Tyson, Manu, Matthew and Luke, you guys are starting."

"We can do this," I yelled, and then we all slapped each other on the back and walked into the center for the tip-off.

We were all jostling for position when the referee was preparing to toss the ball. Seeing the determination on Matthew's face, Tyson and I knew to drop back a little. Sure enough, Matthew tapped the ball straight down to me.

We played like a different team. When the defense was tight everyone ran to get the pass, and Matthew set some great screens, making it possible for us to take the ball to the basket.

I was so relieved watching the last few seconds click down on the clock. When the buzzer went, we were ten points ahead. We all went nuts in celebration.

COACH CLARKE LED US OUT of the stadium and sat us down beneath the shade of a big old gum tree.

"You fellas really got it together against Sydney," he said. "You looked out for each other and were confident in your own ability. And you just beat the team that looked like they were going to be the strongest in the tournament."

"You mean they beat Northern Beaches and Western Sydney?" Manu asked.

"They did, which means if you win your games tomorrow, you're through to the finals."

"Yes!" I said, punching the air. Finally I wasn't regretting that I hadn't just flown to the Torres Strait with Mum and Dad.

"Come on, let's go and cheer the girls on," Coach Clarke instructed.

As everyone shot back into the stadium, Coach pulled me aside. "Patty, I can see that you're hobbling around out there."

I had been so excited by our win, I hadn't really noticed the pain in my ankle. But now that Coach Clarke brought it up, I realized he was right. I wasn't sure exactly

when I'd started limping, but something definitely wasn't right.

I knew what that meant. "But Coach, I'm fine!" I said, knowing he wouldn't be convinced.

"I'm sorry, mate, but I'm going to have to sit you out for a couple of days."

My heart sank to my feet. What was the point of coming to Sydney if I couldn't even play?

Coach Clarke could see how upset I was. "I understand how you feel, Patty. But you need to look after that ankle, or you could do permanent damage. If you take good care of it and rest up – and if we make it to the finals – you could still get back in the game."

WATCHING JOSIE PLAY cheered me up a bit. She swished two three-pointers in a row and Tyson said, "That's how you do it."

"If your hand is hot, keep shooting them," Coach Clarke said. "Don't be afraid to have a go."

On the bus ride back to the boarding school, Tyson sat next to me and said, "I don't know what you did today, but you made us play like a team."

"It was because everyone believed in themselves – it didn't have much to do with me."

"But you helped us believe in ourselves, Patty," he said.

"Lucky everyone has the skills to back it up."

We sat in silence for a while. Finally Tyson said, "Number eight is your number, isn't it, Patty?"

"I wear it for the Shadows."

"You wear it at school too," he pointed out.

"It was my Uncle Sam's number. He always said he wished he had eight arms when he played."

Tyson unzipped his backpack, pulled out his number eight jersey and asked, "Want to swap? You can have it."

Tyson handed me the number eight jersey. "We need you to have eight arms tomorrow, Patty."

I still hadn't told my teammates that I was benched. I wasn't sure how.

I CALLED MUM AND DAD when we got back to the boarding school.

"How's it going?" Dad asked.

"Not too bad," I said. But my voice wasn't convincing.

"What's wrong, Patty?" Mum asked.

"Coach Clarke is benching me for the next couple of games."

"Because of your ankle?"

"It's not that sore," I said.

"Well it must be sore enough for Coach Clarke to bench you," Mum said.

"It's not fair," I said. "I can't play basketball, we've only won one of three games, and I can't be there with you."

"There's got to be some way that you can still help your team, Patty," Dad said.

"From the bench?" I asked.

"Helping your teammates doesn't only happen on the court," Mum said. "I'm sure you'll think of something."

"And don't worry, Patty, you'll be with us before you know it," Dad told me before we said goodbye.

After we'd lined up to get our dinner I sat with Luke and waved Josie and Riley over to sit with us.

"What's up, *bala*?" Josie asked when they sat down.

"Coach Clarke told me I have to sit a couple of games out because of my ankle."

"Oh no," Luke said.

"And our team isn't as strong as yours, Josie."

"But resting your ankle is the most important thing," she reminded me.

"I don't have much choice. But we need something else up our sleeve if we're going to have any chance of making the grand final," I told them.

"Like what?" Josie asked.

"I was hoping to show our team some of our

Shadows set plays, or at least some signals so that people know where to move on the court."

"Yeah, that'd be good," Luke said. I thought he'd be on board – he wanted to win as badly as I did.

Josie shook her head. "But then Tyson and everyone will know our tactics when we start playing against them during the club season."

I nodded while looking each of my Shadows teammates in the eye. "That's what I'm worried about too," I said, "and why I'm asking you guys first. I just figure if I didn't do this I wouldn't be doing my best for Canberra."

Josie shoveled some salad into her mouth as she sat thinking.

Riley broke the silence. "I know what you can

do. You can show your teammates our tactics, but the next time we play against them we change all our signals."

"That sounds good, Patty," Luke said. I looked at Josie to see what she thought. Finally she nodded. "Thank you," I told her, and then left the table to see Coach Clarke.

"WHAT'S UP?" Coach Clarke asked when I tapped him on the shoulder.

"Coach, can we use the court after dinner?"

"I was going to put on a film for everyone."

"I just want to show my teammates a few things," I told him.

"There's no way you're running around though, Patty."

"I promise I won't."

"If that's what the others want, sure, I'm okay with that. But make sure they save some energy for tomorrow."

"Thanks, Coach," I said before going back to the table to finish my dinner.

WE FOLLOWED MR. JONES into the boarding school's gym. The lights buzzed when he switched them on.

"So, why have you dragged us in here?" Tyson asked as I walked onto the court.

"You know how all your club teams used to thrash the Shadows, but then we started beating you?" I asked.

"We only beat you in your first couple of games. Once your team got used to playing together, you were just better than us," Matthew said.

"We won the grand final after you thrashed us at the start of the season," I reminded everyone.

"Do you have to rub it in?" Tyson said.

"How did you guys get so good so quickly?" Matthew asked.

"We used some tricks," Luke blurted out.

Everyone's eyes opened wide. "What kind of tricks?" Matthew asked.

"They're more tactics than tricks. And signals too," I replied. "Here, I'll show you."

To start with I got Matthew to stand near Luke. Walking only, I dribbled the ball toward them and then held up two fingers. Luke burst to the left-hand side of the court, where I passed the ball to him.

"How did Luke know where to run?" Bruce asked.

Luke and I told everyone about the signal we used and what it meant.

"Show us some more," Tyson said, impressed.

"Don't worry, Tyson, I'm going to show you a whole lot in the next hour because it's going to be you calling the shots tomorrow. Coach Clarke has benched me for the next couple of games."

MY TEAM TOOK THE NEWS hard at first. But soon they rallied around me, making me sit and rest my ankle, and promising they would make it to the grand final so that I could play again.

From the sideline, I showed them four basic plays and made them practice each a few times.

About half an hour later, Matthew knew when to fake to the side and cut to the basket. Everyone knew when Tyson was going to shoot a three-pointer and to get ready for rebounds. They also knew the signals for passing the ball to the left and right side of the keyway and to the top of the key.

I'd never seen Tyson concentrate as hard as he did when I ran through the plays. When I passed the ball to him and said, "Your turn to have a go now, Tyson," he dribbled out to the top of the key, determined to get the signals and passes right.

Coach Clarke walked into the gym, clapped when he saw what we were doing and said, "Great work, team! But it's time to get ready for bed now."

When we were all in bed I told everyone, "No talking or messing around tonight. I want us all to get a good sleep for tomorrow. If you can't sleep, think about our plays, and memorize them, because we're going to need them."

Tyson gave me the thumbs-up and when it was lights-out, everyone was silent.

JUST BEFORE WE left the change rooms to play our first of two games for the day, Bruce asked Tyson, "So in what order are you going to give us the signals?"

Before Tyson answered, I said, "It doesn't work like that."

"Yeah, you can't just try a set play every time you go to the basket," Luke said.

"Everyone still needs to try to get in the best position and go with the flow of the game," I said. "But keep your eyes on Tyson and when he sees an opportunity, he'll signal. Then we put our plays into action."

Matthew won the tip-off, tapping it down to Luke. As soon as Luke passed the ball to Tyson he ran his hand across his head, signaling he was going to shoot a three-pointer.

His shot bounced off the ring, but just as we'd practiced, everyone positioned themselves for the rebounds, and Matthew tipped the ball in the basket for two points.

Close to the end of the first half everyone was trying as hard as they could, but also having a lot more fun, even me on the bench, congratulating my teammates when things went right and encouraging them when they needed a boost.

Tyson shot two three-pointers in a row at the beginning of the second half, and Luke brought down a whole heap of rebounds to help us easily beat Newcastle.

"Coach Clarke, please let me play this next game," I said, opening up my backpack and showing him that I'd brought my gear.

"I'm sorry, Patty, you can't risk your ankle," he replied, and I could see that he wouldn't budge.

Luckily our team's confidence continued to grow, and we beat Gosford by twenty-three points. Every time the guys pulled off one of the plays that I'd showed them, Tyson gave me the thumbs-up.

COACH CLARKE WAS the most excited I'd ever seen him after we won that game. "If you guys keep playing like that, you'll win the next game and get through to the tournament grand final.

Canberra has never done that in the thirty years we've competed!"

I had no idea that Canberra had never made it to the grand final before. I knew that my teammates were as excited as I was to become the first Canberra team to get there.

That night I sat right in front of Coach Clarke with an ice pack on my ankle, hoping he'd let me play in the next game.

THE GIRLS PLAYED their first game before ours. Watching them really pumped us up. Their opponents, Sydney, were strong, but Josie and Riley kept running hard and getting in some amazing shots. They were on fire.

When the buzzer went and Canberra won, all the boys and I stood up on the benches and started yelling out "Canberra, Canberra, Canberra!"

Coach Clarke turned to us. "That's the way to do it, boys. Come on, let's get ready."

"What about me, can I get ready too?" I asked.

Coach had been watching me all day, I could tell. "Change into your gear, Patty," he said. "But there's no guarantee of any court time." His face was stern, but my hopes shot up.

I warmed up with the team and couldn't feel any pain in my ankle at all. Everyone was a lot more relaxed than usual, even though Northern Beaches were warming up at the other end of the court.

I didn't know if it was because we were trying to preserve our energy, or if my team was feeling a lot more confident.

I spoke to every player, reminding them of how much stronger we'd grown as a team since Northern Beaches thrashed us at the start of the tournament.

Ten minutes into the first half of our game it was clear how much our team had changed. At halftime, Canberra was winning by twelve points. I was cheering so hard from the bench that my voice went hoarse.

But Northern Beaches started catching up in the second half. Before we knew it, they were leading by four points with only five minutes left.

Coach Clarke called a time-out, turned to me and asked, "Are you sure your ankle is okay, Patty?"

"Good as new," I told him honestly. I hadn't felt so much as a twinge in it.

“I’m sending you on,” he said, and I was flooded with excitement.

When the team was huddled around, Coach said, “You guys were leading by twelve points earlier. Yes, Northern Beaches are playing hard, but you know you have it in you to fight back. Go back out there and find that confidence again.”

I knew I needed to try something to lift my team straightaway. I dribbled the ball down the court and signaled to my teammates that I was lining up for a three-pointer. When I made the shot, they all yelled and punched the air.

After that, my teammates, especially Manu and Bruce, began to take more risks and our game started to flow again.

Josie, Riley and the other Canberra girls were

on the edge of the court in the dying minutes of the game, cheering us on. When the buzzer sounded, we were ahead by six.

I breathed a sigh of relief. The girls came onto the court and slapped us all on the back. Coach Clarke shook our hands. I wanted to let go and celebrate with my team, but knew that it wasn't time to relax yet. I needed to focus on the tournament grand final against Sydney tomorrow.

AFTER WE'D HAD SHOWERS, we gathered at the bus and asked Coach Clarke what the plan was for the rest of the day. I figured we'd return to the boarding school for drills in the gym.

"We're going sightseeing," Coach said.

"What? Really?"

"If you think about the game too much for the next twenty-four hours you'll be too wound up to play well," Mr. Jones explained. "It's time to take your minds off it."

The bus took us to a huge old building set among gardens. As soon as I could make out the writing above the entrance I realized it was the Art Gallery of New South Wales.

"Awesome!" Josie said, but I could see that Tyson and Bruce weren't so impressed. They'd been eyeing the Ferris wheel at Luna Park on the other side of the harbor for days.

We'd all been to the art gallery in Canberra, but this place was massive. Coach Clarke led us through the Australian galleries, giving us time to look before moving on to the European galleries. The paintings were like windows looking back to earlier times.

After that, we walked into a gallery full of the biggest and most colorful Aboriginal dot paintings I'd ever seen.

"What do the dots mean, Patty?" Tyson asked.

"Who cares?" Manu said. "They look amazing."

I answered, "Mum told me they're like maps that represent the land and places that are important to people and their families."

"Oh," said Tyson. "That's cool. Are there any paintings that tell you where to find good bush tucker?"

I laughed and said, "Yeah, there are!"

We walked into another room full of Aboriginal art. At the end I could see something in a glass case that looked familiar. I walked over to the object, realizing it was something from the Torres Strait, but I couldn't work out what. Then I saw the label – it was a Torres Strait hammerhead shark headdress, bigger than any I'd ever seen.

I could see where a dancer places their head between the fins and behind the mouth of the shark. On top of that piece was another hammerhead shark.

I read the information about the artwork, which told me the object was a Beizam (shark) headdress, made by a man called Ken Thaiday from Erub Island in the Torres Strait.

As I admired the artwork, I started missing Mum and Dad and my family.

It was a good thing that my teammates gathered around me then. Bruce asked, "Are they like the sharks that chased your uncle and cousin when you were fishing?"

"They're from the Torres Strait but a bit different from the reef sharks."

"Well, they're cool anyway," Bruce said.

After the gallery we went to a fancy dinner on the wharf, right near the water's edge. As I ate some spaghetti marinara and wondered if there were sharks swimming in the harbor, I thought about how we'd have to play better than we had in any game during the tournament to give ourselves a chance of winning the grand final.

"PATTY, I CAN'T EVEN EAT I'm so nervous," Manu told me at breakfast.

"Make sure you at least drink water," I told him as I grabbed a banana from the breakfast bar.

I was excited. My happiness over being fit to play in the grand final overcame any jitters I might have felt otherwise. The only bad thing was that the girls' team was playing their grand final at the same time as us. That meant that we wouldn't get to see each other's games.

I sat next to Josie on the way to the stadium. "One more game and then we fly to the Torres Strait," she said.

"It'd be better to arrive as champions," I told Josie.

She held her fist up, smiling. "Let's do it then!"

All the other teams we'd competed against during the tournament filled the stands of Olympic Park Stadium. I could feel energy charging through my body as soon as I hit the court.

Coach Clarke instructed us to keep things relaxed during our warm-up, but when he spoke to us before the game he bent down to our level, looked us all in the eye and said, "You've come so far during the tournament. It's your great teamwork that made it possible. All I ask now is that you keep working together as a team and try your best."

"Go, Canberra!" we all called out. Tyson slapped me on the back as I walked out to the center.

As I waited for the tip-off I tried to tell myself it was just an ordinary game. But then I looked up at the shot clock and saw the words *Canberra* and *Sydney*. I knew it was the biggest game of my life. The crowd was already the loudest I had ever heard.

As the ball was tossed up by the ref to start the game, one of the Sydney players elbowed Manu in the side of the head, and the referee called a foul.

We didn't waste any time. Manu passed the ball to me, and I passed to Matthew, who ran in for an easy layup and scored, getting us off to a great start. But when Sydney had possession of the ball, the crowd's cheering was deafening.

It was only when we were well into the first half and leading by ten points that the cheering for Sydney died down.

BY HALFTIME, we were still ten points in front. I didn't know if I should say anything to my team – we were playing so well, and I didn't want to mess things up.

I looked across toward the girls' game and was excited to see them winning, even if it was only by three points. I waited for Josie and Riley to see me and gave them the thumbs-up.

Coach Clarke and Mr. Jones led us away from the court and sat us down, making sure that we were getting plenty to drink. When Coach spoke to us, it was only to highlight the things we'd done well.

But just before the second half began, Coach Clarke said, "Sydney will fight like crazy to get back into the game. If they do, their supporters are going to scream the roof off. Stay confident and don't let them intimidate you."

I walked back onto the court knowing I'd have to step things up.

COACH CLARKE WAS RIGHT. Sydney started coming back against us, and the more they scored, the louder their fans cheered.

Then Sydney hit the front, and despite what Coach Clarke had told us about staying confident, I could see that my team was anxious – and this was causing us to make mistakes.

When Sydney snuck in front by another two points, Coach Clarke called a time-out. He subbed me off, when I wanted to be on the court more than anything, trying my heart out. “Catch your breath, Patty,” was all that Coach Clarke said.

It was almost impossible to stay still. The only positive of sitting on the bench was that I was able to check the score of the girls' game and see that they were leading by six.

Finally, Coach Clarke turned to me and said, "Patty, go back out there and rev everyone up."

When I got my hands on the ball I kept hold of it for as long as I could, dribbling around players and waiting for an opportunity to make something happen.

Finally I found some space deep on the side of the court. I took a shot from the three-point line and punched the air as I watched the ball swish through the net.

"Come on, Canberra, let's take them on," I yelled.

After we hit the lead again I thought that if we just kept up our intensity we would win.

But suddenly Sydney were two points ahead. There were only a few minutes left on the clock.

I passed the ball to Manu, and he sprinted down the court and passed to Tyson, who scored with a sneaky shot from under the basket.

Yes, I thought, *we've got it!* But somehow Sydney wove the ball through our defense in a flash and scored another two points. I looked at the clock as the Sydney players rushed back. I passed the ball to Matthew but, desperate to get to it, he pushed a player. The referee called the foul and turned the ball over to Sydney.

The Sydney supporters went nuts. I ordered my team into defense and told myself that we could still win.

As the Sydney player passed the ball in to one of their forwards, I saw Tyson racing to intercept the ball. I started running toward our basket. Tyson leapt through the air then passed the ball to me in one quick motion.

I caught the ball and dribbled as fast as I could toward the basket with all the Sydney players chasing me.

I knew I could make a layup and score two points to tie the game. Instead, I attempted a transition jump shot from the three-point line.

I clenched my fists and gritted my teeth as I watched the ball sail through the air.

It swished through the basket.

"Yes!" I yelled, punching the air, just as the buzzer sounded.

I turned to see my teammates running toward me, grinning like maniacs, hands raised in the air.

ON THE BUS to Sydney Airport, Riley and Josie told me about the highlights of their grand final. They had won by eight points. Luke and Manu grimaced as they told the girls how our grand final had almost slipped away from us.

Manu told them how I'd won the game with my jump shot, and I said, "But I could only do it because of Tyson's amazing intercept."

Mr. Jones parked the bus in one of the big airport parking bays, and took my bag and Josie's out from the compartment below.

When we were called to board the plane Coach Clarke said, "Thank you, Patty. We won the tournament not only because you're a great player, but because you helped us become a great team." He shook my hand and said, "Have a terrific holiday, mate, you deserve it!"

All our friends gave us hugs, and when we were almost through the gate, Tyson called out, "Bring me back some bush tucker, Patty."

"And watch out for the sharks!" added Bruce.

Josie and I only took off our tournament medals when we walked through the security scanner.

I FELT SO GROWN UP when I was in the air with Josie. It was so much fun looking down at the clouds.

We changed onto a smaller plane in Cairns, and when we were back in the air again, Josie asked, “Patty, what do you want to do when you’re older?”

After winning the tournament, I didn’t even have to think about it. “I want to train at the Australian Institute of Sport like my uncle,” I said. “And I want to play basketball in the NBA and for Australia at the Olympics.”

“That sounds awesome, Patty,” Josie said. “I think you will.”

The plane started to descend. "Check it out, Patty," Josie said, and we pushed our faces up against the window to see the waters and reefs of the Torres Strait shining blue and green beneath the sun.

I couldn't wait to land, to see Mum and Dad, to celebrate Athe's birthday with my family, to go swimming with my cousins, and to have a milkshake or two at Uncle Frankie's Café, "The Best Shakes in the Straits."

GLOSSARY

Aboriginal: Aborigines. People Indigenous to Australia.

Athe: grandpa. Language of Torres Strait Islander people.

bala: brother. Language of Torres Strait Islander people.

basketballer: a basketball player.

boomer: a male kangaroo.

bush tucker: plants and animals traditionally taken from the land and the sea and cooked in special ways by Aboriginal and Torres Strait Islander people.

centimeter: a little less than half an inch.

change rooms: locker rooms.

footy: short for football. "Footy" means the game of Australian Rules (Aussie rules) football and the ball itself. The ball and the field are oval shaped.

grand final: the last game in a championship series.

have a go: take a chance; give it a try.

hit the front: took the lead.

holidays: vacation.

meter: about 39 inches.

oval: a playing field or sports field for Australian Rules (Aussie rules) football and other sports, including cricket.

Torres Strait: the waters and group of islands between Australia and Papua New Guinea, the traditional home of Torres Strait Islander people. Australia has two Indigenous groups, Aboriginal and Torres Strait Islander.

Torres Strait Islander: Torres Strait Islander people, Indigenous to Australia.

PATTY MILLS was born in Canberra. His father is from the Torres Strait Islands, and his mother is originally from the Kokatha people in South Australia. Patty plays with the San Antonio Spurs in the NBA and is a triple Olympian with the Australian Boomers (Beijing '08, London '12, Rio de Janeiro '16).

JARED THOMAS is a Nukunu person of the Southern Flinders Ranges. His novels include *Dallas Davis, the Scientist and the City Kids* for children, and *Sweet Guy, Calypso Summer* and *Songs that Sound Like Blood* for young adults. Jared's writing explores the power of belonging and culture.